LAURA OWEN & KORKY PAUL

Winnie AND

WINNIE
Goes
Wild

OXFORD
UNIVERSITY PRESS

CONTENTS

Woolly
WILBUR

WINNIE
Goes Wild

Detective
WINNIE

'Ooo, Wilbur!' Winnie clutched poor
Wilbur as if he was a cushion. She peeped
around him at the television. 'That poor
lady has been kidnapped! She's been tied
like a sweet flea plant to a stake, and she
can't escape! Ooo, whatever is going to
happen to her?'

'Mrrugug!' gurgled poor Wilbur.

On the television, Detective Derek had
found Bad Boris in his woodland den.

'Where have you hidden her, Boris? That handbag doesn't go with your outfit, so I know it isn't yours. It must be stolen. It's hers, isn't it! But what have you done with her, eh?'

'Shan't tell!' said Bad Boris.

'Oh poor lady!' said Winnie.

But cunning Detective Derek was already solving the crime.

'Those are strange footprints, Bad Boris,' he said. 'Your left footprints are blue while your right ones are yellow. So I reckon you've got her in that old paint factory!'

'It's true, I have!' wailed Bad Boris.

So the lady was rescued from the paint factory, and given back her handbag. Winnie turned off the televison.

'He's as clever as a clog, that Detective Derek!' said Winnie.

9

The next morning Winnie and Wilbur were in the village when...

'Yap yap yap!'

'Whatever's that?' said Winnie. 'Oo, look, Wilbur! There's a dear little doggy tied up to that post, just like the lady on the telly. He must have been dognapped by a baddie like Bad Boris!'

'Meeo!' Wilbur was shaking his head.

YAP YAP
YAP YAP
YAP
YAP
YAP

'We must save him!' said Winnie.
'That's what Detective Derek would do!'

So Winnie untied the little dog, and
popped it into her shopping bag. Then
they went home. **Yarooo! Yap yap
yap!** noises came from the bag.

'He's just upset by being dognapped,'
said Winnie.

Back home, Winnie took the dog from the bag.

'Grrr snap!'

'You're not a crocodile, so stop that!' said Winnie, snatching her fingers out of the dog's way. 'You're frightened, aren't you, you poor little pooch?'

Winnie offered the dog a bowl of bat's milk.

'Grrr!'

'Would a big brave kind of a name help you?' said Winnie. 'I'm going to call you Butch.'

'Grrr!' said Butch. **'Yap yap yap!'**

Winnie covered her ears. 'We'd better get detecting, and find out where Butch really belongs. Then we can give him back to his grateful owner. Get thinking like a detective, Wilbur! Baddies like Boris live in woodland lairs so that's where we'll go.

Winnie grabbed everything they might need for detective work: a magnifying glass, a torch, a scribble-book, and some jam jars for samples.

'**Yap yap yap!**' said Butch as Winnie
and Wilbur shut him in the house. They
got on to the broom.

'We must go to the woods!' said Winnie,
and off they flew until they landed with a
bump in the middle of a clump of trees.

'Can you see any bad burglar types?'
Winnie asked Wilbur. **Squelch!** One of
Winnie's shoes had fallen off. **Hop-bop**
hop-bop. She used her broom as a
crutch as she hopped to a log and put the
shoe back on.

They made their way through the wood,
peering and listening and sniffing for clues
but they only found twigs and leaves and
rabbit poos. Soon they were back in the
village. And there they did find a clue!

'A footprint!' said Winnie. 'That's
just the sort of clue we need! Oo, there's
another one! Very suspicious! I reckon
they must belong to a burglar!'

Winnie took a deep breath. 'We've got
to be as brave as a chicken asking a fox for
a dance now, Wilbur. Come on!'

The suspicious footprints led Winnie and Wilbur straight back to the wood.

'I *knew* we'd find our burglar in the wood,' said Winnie. But then, 'Ooer, that's strange,' said Winnie. 'There's only a left footprint here. A left footprint, then another left footprint, then a little round thing instead of a right footprint. Oo, I know what that means!'

'Meow?' said Wilbur.

'It means that our dog-napper is someone with a wooden leg. A pirate!'

Then the footprints with the wooden-leg prints stopped. 'So where is the pilfering pirate?' said Winnie. They couldn't find him in the wood, and there were no other clues to follow, so they flew home.

A lot of howling was coming from
Winnie's house.

'Poor little Butchy,' said Winnie. Then
she noticed the suspicious footprints
outside her house.

'Oh, no!' she screeched, 'the pirate must
be inside my house!' Winnie picked up
Wilbur and clutched him like a cushion
again. 'No wonder little Butchy is howling!'

Wilbur jumped down and pointed to
where Winnie had just taken a step . . .
leaving a suspicious footprint from
her shoe.

'Oo, Wilbur!' said Winnie. 'You don't
think . . . ?'

'Meow!' nodded Wilbur.

'So we've been tracking *me* all along?'
said Winnie. 'I am the pirate?' Gulp! went
Winnie. 'I never knew I was a pirate! So,
oh golly-mollykins, I didn't rescue Butch,
at all. I dog-napped him! Oo, Wilbur,
maybe his owner was inside the shop all
along? Er, do you think we can sneak
Butch back before anybody notices?'

They popped Butch back into Winnie's
bag, and they flew back to the shop.
Winnie was just tying Butch back to the
lamp post when Winnie's sister Wilma
burst out of the shop.

23

'Oh, Winnie, you've *found* my little
darling!' said Wilma, pouncing on Butch.

'I didn't mean to dog-nap him . . .'
began Winnie. Then she realized what
Wilma had said. 'Er, that's right, Wilma,'
said Winnie. 'I found Butch. That's what
I did. Is he yours, Wilma?'

'She's a *she*, not a *he*!' said Wilma. 'She's called Fluffball.'

'Fluffball!' said Winnie.

'Me-he-he!' said Wilbur.

'Grrr! Yap!' said Fluffball-Butch.

'I think she's saying "thank you, Auntie Winnie",' cooed Wilma.

'Mmm,' said Winnie and she left, rather quickly.

25

'I don't speak Dog,' said Winnie
when they got home, 'but I think that
Fluffball was saying something as rude as
a barnacle's bottom to us back there, and
not "thank you" at all!'

'Meow?' said Wilbur.

'I do understand Cat, though,' said
Winnie. 'Yes, let's have that nice cup of
stink-weed tea and an evil-weevil biscuit.
We're just in time for the next Detective
Derek Mystery on the telly.'

28

WINNIE'S
Different Day

Winnie's alarm croc snapped its teeth.

Snip-snap, snip-snap!

'Get up Winniiee. Get up, Wilburr!' it
snapped, just as it did every day.

'All right, half left!' grumbled Winnie.
'I'm getting out of bed, aren't I?' Winnie
tipped out of her bed on the right side,
just as she always did. She shoved her feet
into her slip-sloppers, first the left one
then the right one, just as she always did.

She went to the bathroom and she was just washing her face in the same sort of way as she always did when a thought hit her like a slap round the cheeks with a wet fish.

'You know what, Wilbur?' said Winnie, splashing her hands into the soapy water in the sink. 'I'm bored with doing the same ordinary things in the same ordinary-as-a-centipede-running-out-of-socks way, day after day after day.'

Wilbur licked his right paw and stroked it over his head, then lifted his left leg to have a wash under that.

'And you're just as boring as I am! You always do that while I'm washing my face!' Wilbur stopped still, leg in the air, tongue hanging out.

'Go on. Finish doing it,' said Winnie.
'You enjoy tasting all those fur flavours.
And I've got to wash my face otherwise
there will be sleepy bits in my eyes all day
long.'

32

Winnie spoke to her back-to-front
self in the mirror. 'We do have to do the
ordinary things, but we don't have to do
them in ordinary ways, do we? Let's have a
Doing Things Differently Day today!'

So Winnie put her dress on back to front. That felt new and interesting. She combed all the tangles out of her hair and plaited it neatly. It did look *very* different. She walked backwards instead of forwards down the stairs—**bump! crash!** She ate her breakfast porridge with a fork instead of a spoon, and she put pepper and mustard on it instead of sweet-bug syrup.

'Very nice!' said Winnie.

Then she hopped upstairs and brushed her teeth, holding the brush in her right hand instead of her left and starting from the opposite side to normal.

She got ready to go out. 'We do need to get a few bits and blobs of shopping, Wilbur. Fetch the bags, will you, and I'll get my broom and purse.'

35

Winnie and Wilbur sat backwards on
the broom to be different. It was a rather
uncomfortable way to be different. When
they got to the shop, Winnie gave the
shopkeeper her list.

'Biscuits, bread, bin liners, bunion
cream,' he read, in a boringly ordinary
voice.

'What a boringly ordinary list!' said Winnie. Then Winnie noticed some little ordinaries who didn't seem to be finding their shopping ordinary or boring at all.

'One of those!'

'A bag of them!'

'What sort of shopping are you doing?' Winnie asked them.

'We've each got thirteen pence pocket
money to spend,' explained one little
ordinary. 'We're choosing which sweets
to buy. There are jelly snakes, fizzy dabs,
scrunch munch pellets, biteable bead
bangles, gob stoppers, milk bottles, liquorice
laces, sherbet bombs, chewy strawberries,
chocolate bars, trillions and billions . . .'

'Ooh, pocket money sounds fun to
spend.' Winnie opened her toad purse.
'I've only got boring ordinary money
in my purse. Where do you get pocket
money from?'

'We earn it by doing little jobs,' the
little ordinaries told her.

So Winnie and Wilbur went off to do
some little jobs.

Winnie tried busking. But she was
so out of tune that no-one gave her any
money.

Then Winnie tried cleaning windscreens.
But she forgot to ask people to close their
windows before she threw her bucket of
water.

'You'll have to pay me for the damage!'
said a cross, soggy driver.

40

Then Winnie set up a stall selling hop-corn flop-corn plop-corn rot-corn not-corn, but nobody bought any at all.

Wilbur did some little jobs, too.

He caught mice, he warmed knees, he polished anything that needed polishing.

'I haven't earned anything!' sighed weary Winnie.

'Meeow!' Wilbur proudly held out his
coins.

'Yippee!' Winnie danced a little dance.
'Clever you, Wilbur! Now we've got lots
of pocket money!'

'Meow!' Wilbur turned Winnie around
to make her look away from him, then he
hid coins here and there and everywhere
and turned Winnie back to look.

'Where have all the coins gone?' said
Winnie. 'Ooh, I see! It's a pocket-money
treasure hunt!' And off she scampered,
peering and pouncing and picking up coins.

The little ordinaries joined the treasure
hunt and they all found coins, too. Then
they all went pocket-money shopping
together.

'Oh, this is much more fun than ordinary shopping!' said Winnie. 'I'll have three humming bugs, and one rubble gum, and one big gob slobber, please. Oh, and a fizzy fish and two mint mice for Wilbur.'

Winnie and Wilbur walked home,
scoffing sweets.

'Different is good!' sighed Winnie—
chew! scrunch! munch! 'And sweets
are nice. But now I fancy something fresh
and juicy. Can you guess what I'm going
to do with my last pocket-money penny,
Wilbur?'

'Meow?' Wilbur shook his head.

'I'm going to throw it into that wishing well!' **Plop!** went the penny. Then Winnie closed her eyes and wished as hard as she could.

'Meow?' said Wilbur, pointing at Winnie's wand.

'Oh I know,' said Winnie, opening one eye. 'But I can do *that* sort of magic any old day, and I'm doing things differently today, remember? Now, let me wish my wish.'

PLOP!

And suddenly—**splat-splat-splat!**—it was raining pong berries, just as Winnie had wished for! She held out her shopping bag to catch them.

'Well, that *was* a different sort of shopping!' laughed Winnie, stuffing purple pong berries into her mouth.

'When we get home, Wilbur, I'm going to sleep upside down in my bed, to be different. Then tomorrow we'll go back to being ordinary. But all the ordinary things will feel nice and different because we've had a holiday from them. That's a kind of magic!'

Woolly
WILBUR

Winnie woke-up with a blue nose with icicle drips on the end of it. Her teeth were clacking like tap-dancing skeletons. The only bit of her that was warm was her tummy, and that was because fat furry Wilbur was curled up, purring on top of it.

'It's s-s-so c-c-cold!' said Winnie. 'We'd b-b-better g-g-get up, Wilbur. L-l-light the f-f-fire to w-w-warm the house.'

53

Winnie got dressed fast, then she
and Wilbur hurried downstairs. Drifty-
draughty cold winds whistled under
Winnie's doors and around Winnie's
windows and up her skirt.

'I need a n-n-nice big m-m-mug of c-c-
cocoa!' said Winnie, licking her lips at the
thought of that sweet, smooth, chocolaty
taste running down through her body
pipes like a radiator system to warm her
from the inside.

'M-m-meow!' agreed Wilbur. He pulled
open the fridge door, but, 'Mrrrow!'

'No milk?' said Winnie. 'Oh, bats'
bottoms, that means no hot chocolate!
And I so fancy a drink of hot chocolate!
We'll just have to go and buy some milk.'

Winnie opened the front door.

'Look, it's snowing!' said Winnie. 'Where in this w-w-white world are our w-w-woollies, Wilbur?'

Wilbur pulled open the door of the cupboard under the stairs, and out flew four fat happily chomping moths.

'Those mean moths have munched our mittens to bits!' wailed Winnie. 'They've hogged our hats and snacked on our scarves! Oh, Wilbur, we can't go out in this snowy cold without woollies to keep us warm. We'd freeze as solid as frog fingers fresh from the freezer!'

'Meow?' suggested Wilbur, doing some strange movements with his paws.

'Good idea!' said Winnie. 'We just need to find some wool, and then I'll knit-knot some lovely new warm winter woollies for us to wear!'

But when they opened the wool cupboard, out flew five even fatter moths!

'You greedy, gobbling, fluttering, stealing, miserable moths!' Winnie was jumping up and down with rage, trying to whack the moths, but they flittered away and she only whacked the ornaments and poor Wilbur. 'How on earth are we going to get wool to knit some woollies to keep us warm enough to go out into the snow to walk to the shop to buy some milk to make hot chocolate, eh?'

Wilbur shrugged, but Winnie's face
was suddenly stretching into a big smile.
She pulled her wand from her pocket. 'Of
course!' she said. 'What we need is sheep!
A flock of fat fluffy sheep!' Winnie waved
her wand. *Abracadabra!*

For a moment or two it seemed as if no magic had happened. But when Winnie opened the front door to check if there were any sheep on the doorstep, Wilbur pointed to the sky. A flurry of snow was falling, falling, falling in that way that makes you feel dizzy.

'Waddling wombats!' said Winnie. 'I've never seen such big snowflakes!'

Then Wilbur jumped out of the way
just in time as—**thump!**—a sheep landed
where he had been standing. **Thump!**
Thump! More and more sheep landed in
the snow by the doorway, and then they
baa-rged their way into the house.

'Well,' said Winnie. 'I ordered a flock of sheep, so they've flown down like a flock of birds! Shut the door, Wilbur, and let's get shearing!'

It was quite fun clipping the sheep into interesting shapes. Not as much fun for the sheep, of course. Wilbur made his sheep look odd. Winnie made her sheep look very, very odd.

63

But they soon had a pile of what looked
like dirty candy floss.

'It's got to be spun into balls of wool
before we can knit with it,' said Winnie.
'Spindly-spiders are the best spinners.'
Winnie waved her wand. '*Abracadabra!*'

Instantly there were spiders, with lots of
legs wriggle-spinning the fluffy wool.

'Hold out your arms, Wilbur!' said
Winnie. 'Now we need to wind the wool.'

Then, at last, they were ready to start
knitting.

'Well,' said Winnie. 'All that work
has warmed me up a bit, but it's made
me thirsty too. I really, really want a big
bubbling mug of hot chocolate more than
ever now, so let's knit really, really fast!'

65

Winnie tried knitting with broom handles. 'The fatter the needles are, the faster the knitting grows,' she said. 'I'm making you a tail warmer, Wilbur!' **Knit knit, clickety-click!**

But Winnie's knitting was just too big! 'This is no good, it's like a flipping fisherman's net!' said Winnie. 'You can't wear this, Wilbur!'

'I'll try knitting with wands instead,'
said Winnie. **Knit knit, clickety-click!** 'Ah, that's much better!'

Winnie knitted hats and gloves and
tail warmers and scarves and ponchos.

'Meow!' said Wilbur, pointing to the clock.

'That's true,' said Winnie. 'We'd better go and get that milk before the shops shut.'

So they put on all their new woollies, and they opened the front door, and ... didn't go anywhere because there was a white wall of snow completely filling the doorway. 'We're trapped!' wailed Winnie. 'Oh no! And I do so want a drink of hot chocolate!'

68

Wilbur dug the snow. Winnie shovelled
the snow. But they couldn't shovel a path
all the way into the village in time before
the shops shut.

'I know what we can do,' said Winnie. She took off her tights (she had two pairs on!). Then she tied them to her knitted netting and fixed everything to the gate posts. 'There!' she said.

'Meow?' asked Wilbur.

'It's a catapult!' said Winnie. 'A catapult to hurl you all the way to the shops to get some milk!'

70

'Mrrooww!' protested Wilbur, but
Winnie was already loading him, along with
a bag and purse, into the catapult.

Tug tug twang!

Neeeoow! Wilbur shot over the snow
to land—**flump!**—just outside the shop.

'Yay, that looks fun!' said the little
ordinaries. 'How did you do that, Wilbur?'

The little ordinaries waited for Wilbur
to get the milk, then they dug him a path
back to Winnie's house so that they could
all take it in turns to be catapulted—
flump!—into the snow. And Winnie
brewed a whole cauldron of hot chocolate
for everyone to share.

'With lovely toasted-ant hundreds
and thousands sprinkles and mushroom-
mallows!' said Winnie.

The little ordinaries were so very
grateful for the goes on the catapult that
they said that Winnie should have all
the sprinkles and mushroom-mallows
on her cup, and they didn't take any for
themselves. 'Aren't they such nice-as-lice
little ordinaries?' said Winnie, resting her
feet up on a nice warm sheep.

WINNIE
Goes Wild

'Winnie, are you listening to me?'
screeched Winnie's sister Wendy down
the telling moan. 'I don't want you
embarrassing me in front of my friends.
It's a barbecue with an exotic theme so
you've got to look *exotic!* OK?'

'I haven't got anything exotic to wear,'
said Winnie, who wasn't at all in the mood
for one of Wendy's parties.

'See you at six,' nagged Wendy. **Click!**

And that was the end of the moan call.

'**Mnfff,**' said Winnie from under
the frantically frilly party frock she was
struggling to put on.

'Meow?' asked Wilbur as he watched
Winnie wriggling into her dress.

'I said that I think it's going to rain and
make the sausages squelchy at Wendy's
barbecue,' huffed Winnie, popping her
head through the party frock neck. She

pulled the dress down, and looked at
herself in the mirror. 'Not very exotic, is it?'
Winnie waved her wand. *Abracadabra!*

And instantly, there on her head, was a
hat made of pineapple and bananas and
grapes. It wobbled, but the grapes were tasty.

'Yum!' said Winnie, popping a grape into her mouth. 'We'd better get going, Wilbur, before I eat all my hat.'

They climbed aboard Winnie's broom, and took off, up into the cloudy sky.

'Ooer!' said Winnie as the broom swerved this way and that in the wiffly-waffly wind. Wilbur closed his eyes and held on tight. The wind whipped Winnie's hat ribbons undone and tossed the fruit from her head. 'Oh, no!' wailed Winnie as rain began to splatter. Soon Wilbur was a soggy cat, and Winnie was a drippy witch. Then it began to hail. **Ping ping!** Cold hard pellets pelted them.

'Ow! Ow!' said Winnie.

'Me-Ow! Me-Ow!' said Wilbur.

But just then the wind suddenly blew
them into a big billowing blue-black cloud
that rumbled thunder around them and
bumped them about.

'Wilburrr!' shouted Winnie as she fell
off her broom . . . down through the soft
wet cloud.

'Grab hold of my hand, Wilbur!'
shouted Winnie, and, paw-in-hand, they
fell together down through the cloud.
Then down through the trees, which
ripped and snagged their clothes as they
fell, until finally they landed with a bump
on the ground.

'Where in the whoopsy-world are we?'
wondered Winnie.

'Hiss!'

81

'It's no good hissing about it, Wilbur,' began Winnie. But then, 'Oh,' she said. It wasn't Wilbur who was hissing. **Clack clack clack!** Wilbur's knees knocked together because a huge snake was slithering past them!

Chit chat! went a monkey.
Squawk! went a bright birdie.
Steam! went the air all around.

82

'Uh-oh,' said Winnie. 'I think we've landed in a jungle! What are we going to do about Wendy's party? She's going to be a crotchety-cross witch if we're late! Or if we're not looking right.' Winnie looked at Wilbur. 'Oh, dear, you are one mega-messy moggy. You look as if you've been dragged through a tree backwards. I can't take you to Wendy's looking like that! You need a wash!'

'Mrrow!' protested Wilbur, as
Winnie picked him up and dangled
him over a marshy pool of green water.
Then, **'Urgh!'** said Winnie. There was
something hideously horrible in the water!
'Whatever can that be?'

The horrible thing in the water
wobbled, talking silently as Winnie talked
out loud. 'Oh, no!' screeched Winnie. The
horrible thing was her own reflection!

'I look worse than you do, Wilbur!'
said Winnie.

But, just then, the reflected Winnie
wobbled and—*snap!*—up came the
jaws of an alligator! The alligator fancied
Wilbur's furry worm of a tail for his tea!

Winnie whipped out her wand, and waved it, '**Abracadabra!**' And instantly the last ribbon holding up what was left of her ragged party dress whirled from her waist, and it tied the alligator's jaws tight in a big pink bow.

'**Sngrr!**' went the alligator.

'The ribbon won't hold for long!' warned Winnie. 'Run for it!'

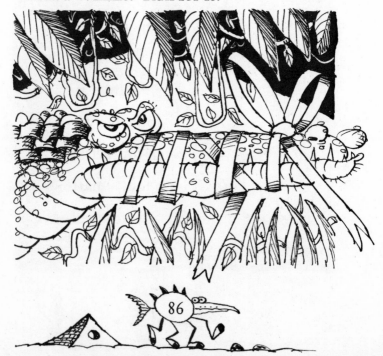

Winnie scrabbled up a tree. Very soon
she was surrounded by monkeys. They
were poking and scratching and **ooh-
ooh-ooh-ing.**

'Wilbur!' said Winnie. 'Where are you?'

Then Winnie saw Wilbur. He was
padding along the branch towards her.

'Ooh, Wilbur, you do look smart!' said
Winnie. 'How did you tidy yourself up so
quickly?'

'**Purrr!**' went Wilbur as he padded
closer. His purr was louder and lower than
usual. The branch bent under the weight
of his sleek black body.

'Er, Wilbur?' said Winnie. 'Um, what
big paws you've got, Wilbur. What
big eyes you've got, Wilbur. Oh, no!

Oh, help!' shouted Winnie because she suddenly realized that this Wilbur wasn't Wilbur after all! This was a panther, and it was opening its toothy greedy grin as it got ready to pounce on her . . .

Just as—'Mrrow!'—real, dear Wilbur
was swinging through the trees with a
troop of monkeys who snatched Winnie to
safety.

It was rather nice being swung through
the trees, nearly naked. Winnie and Wilbur
collected things as they went. **Whoops!**
—some leaves— **whoops!**—some
feathers—**whoops!**—some nuts and
flowers and fruits and vines and jungle
bugs.

By the time they came down to land,
Winnie's and Wilbur's legs were like jelly,
but they had collected enough things to
make an exotic outfit for Winnie, with just
one wave of her wand. *Abradcadabra!*
All ready for Wendy's party,' said Winnie.

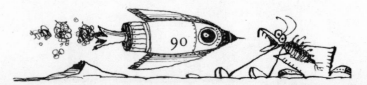

The monkeys brought them their broom, and soon they were flying up and out of the jungle.

The stormy weather had cleared, and
they landed in Wendy's garden just as
Wendy was checking her watch.

'We're here!' shouted Winnie. 'And
we've brought you some exotic fruits and
exotic nuts for your exotic party.' Winnie
handed over their plate of jungle goodies.
Then she collapsed into a deckchair, with
a happy sigh.

'But . . .' said Wendy, her eyes popping and her mouth dropping open in surprise. 'You look exceptionally, extremely, extraordinarily exotic! You told me that you hadn't got anything exotic to wear, Winnie! So where did you get your outfit?'

'Oh, we went a bit wild and picked these things up in a jungle-sale,' said Winnie. *Abracadabra!* Winnie casually waved her wand, and her broom instantly burst into exotic flowers.

'Now, that's just showing off!' said Wendy.

Enjoy more magic moments with
Winnie and **Wilbur**